The Very Best Daddy of ALL

The Very Best Daddy of ALL

by **Marion Dane Bauer**

illustrated by **Leslie Wu**

Simon & Schuster Books for Young Readers

New York   London   Toronto   Sydney   Singapore

Simon & Schuster Books for Young Readers

An imprint of Simon & Schuster Children's Publishing Division

1230 Avenue of the Americas, New York, New York 10020

Text copyright © 2004 by Marion Dane Bauer

Illustrations copyright © 2004 by Leslie Wu

Book design by Mark Siegel

The text for this book is set in Garamond.

The illustrations for this book are rendered in pastel.

Manufactured in China

6 8 10 9 7

Library of Congress Cataloging-in-Publication Data

Bauer, Marion Dane.

The very best daddy of all / by Marion Dane Bauer ; illustrated by Leslie Wu.—1st ed.

p. cm.

Summary: Pictures and rhyming text show how some fathers, animal, bird, and human, take care of their children
by bringing them food, playing with them, and keeping them safe.

ISBN 0-689-84178-7

[1. Father and child—Fiction. 2. Animals—Fiction. 3. Stories in rhyme.] I. Wu, Leslie, ill. II. Title.

PZ8.3.B3199 Ve 2004

[E]—dc21   2001042979

To Peter,
the very best daddy of all

—M. D. B.

To my father, who, when I was young,
brought me to the Adirondacks to show me the beauty

—L. W.

Some daddies
sing you awake.

Some bring
breakfast,
crunchy and sweet.

Some daddies
comb your hair,
gently, gently,
so you'll be fresh
and neat.

Some daddies
build you a house.

Some play
with you too.

Some take care
of your mama,
so she can
take care of you.

Some daddies come when you're lost.

Some hold you
snug and tight.

Some daddies
face every danger,
so you will be
all right.

Some daddies call,
"Keep trying!
Keep trying!"

Some comfort you
when you are crying.

Some daddies
stay close beside you,
whether you're fast
or slow.

Some tuck you in,
safe and warm,
when the sun's
about to go.

And my daddy . . .
haven't you guessed?
From all of the daddies,
tall or small,
mine is the best,
the very best,

the very best
daddy of all.

I go to the garden and talk to a Peacock.

"Not mine," says the Peacock.
He gives me a feather and shakes his blue head.
"Mine have all colors, but not one is so red."

I ask a Magician to show me some magic.

"Can you bring back the bird
who has lost this red feather?"

He waves his big arms. "I cannot do that.
Only very white doves come out of my hat."

Then he gives me a feather and wishes me luck.

The mountain is high and Marlene comes with me.

An Eagle flies down to ask why we are there.
"We want the red bird who lost this red feather."

"Red birds don't fly this high in the sky.
No red feathers here," he says, and bends down
to give us a feather that's a very nice brown.

We ride down the cliffs to the edge of the sea.
We call to the gulls and they fly close to me.

"Not ours," say the gulls. "Our feathers are gray."
They add one to the others and we go on our way.

A Pirate has come from lands that are far.
He says he can't take us to where red birds are.

"My boat is a wreck, I'm tired and old.
I'm looking for someplace to bury my gold.

"That feather," he says, "is from no bird I've seen
Have one from my parrot. It's a very bright green."

We give up the search. The red bird can't be found.

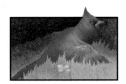

Going home through the woods, I see on the ground
a red cardinal crying and hopping around.

"I've got your lost feather. There's no need to cry."

But the red bird says sadly: "It won't help, I can't fly.
I need more than a feather. I've broken my wing.
I'm so hurt and so hungry, I can't even sing."

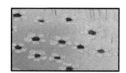

I ask Marlene to help and we work hard together,
We build a bird's nest and put in every feather.

We feed him and nurse him until he can fly.

Then we call all our friends to wave him good-bye.

For Manon

© **1994, Gilles Tibo**

Published in Canada by Tundra Books, Montreal, Quebec H3Z 2N2

Published in the United States by Tundra Books of Northern New York, Plattsburg, N.Y. 12901

Library of Congress Catalog Number: 94-60134

Canadian Cataloging in Publication Data
Tibo, Gilles, 1951-.
        [Simon et la plume perdue. English]
    Simon finds a feather

ISBN 0-88776-340-5

[Issued also in French under title: *Simon et la plume perdue* ISBN 0-88776-341-3]

        I. Title. II. Title: Simon et la plume perdue. English.

PS8589.I26S53414 1994   jC843'.54   C94-900183-X
PZ7.T43Si 1994

The publisher has applied funds from its Canada Council block grant for 1994 toward the editing and production of this book.

Printed in Hong Kong by South China Printing Co. Ltd.